GASTON GOES to the KENTUCKY DERBY

GASTON GOES to the KENTUCKY DERBY

Written and Illustrated by
JAMES RICE

PELICAN PUBLISHING COMPANY
Gretna 1994

Copyright ©1994
By James Rice
All rights reserved

Library of Congress Cataloging-in-Publication Data

Rice, James, 1934-
    Gaston goes to the Kentucky Derby / written and illustrated by
James Rice.
        p. cm.
    Summary: Gaston the alligator and Black Lightning the horse leave
the bayou to compete in the Kentucky Derby.
    ISBN 1-56554-065-4
    [1. Alligators—Fiction. 2. Horses—Fiction. 3. Horse racing-
-Fiction. 4. Stories in rhyme.] I. Title.
PZ8.3.R36Garb 1994
[E]—dc20   94-2196
                                                          CIP
                                                          AC

*The words "Churchill Downs," the "Kentucky Derby," and the replication
of the "Twin Spires" are registered trademarks of Churchill Downs
Incorporated, and are used herein with the permission of Churchill
Downs.*

Printed in Korea

Published by Pelican Publishing Company, Inc.
1101 Monroe Street, Gretna, Louisiana 70053

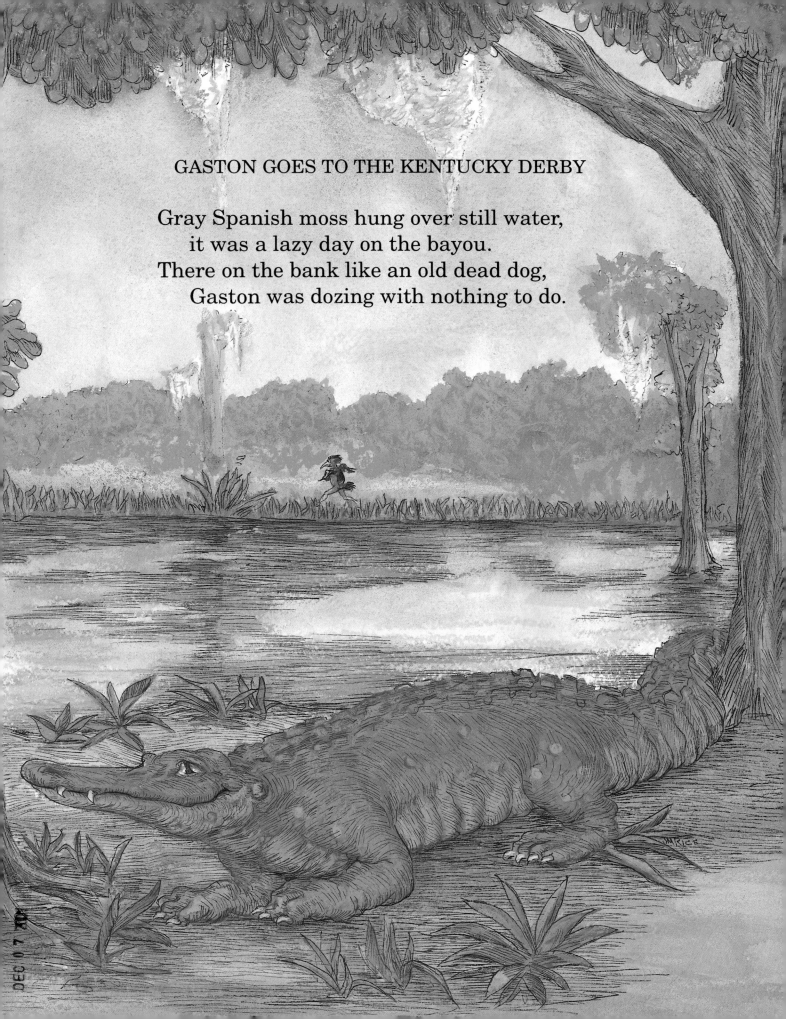

GASTON GOES TO THE KENTUCKY DERBY

Gray Spanish moss hung over still water,
it was a lazy day on the bayou.
There on the bank like an old dead dog,
Gaston was dozing with nothing to do.

Through the trees he saw a great stallion
with long legs and black as the night,
His head high and legs all aquiver,
he was poised and ready for flight.

Black Lightning loved to run,
  he lived up to his name.
Some day winning races
  would be his claim to fame.

The local races soon were all won—
  they faced no competition.
They traveled north to Kentucky
  to the best race in the nation.

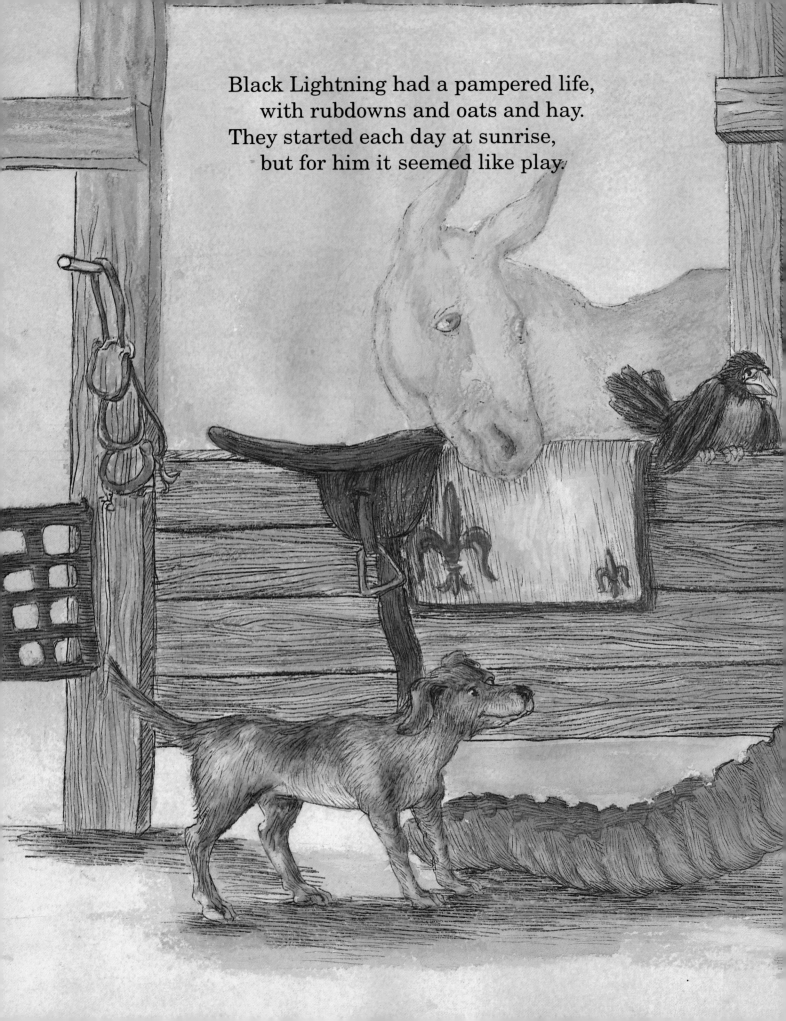

Black Lightning had a pampered life,
with rubdowns and oats and hay.
They started each day at sunrise,
but for him it seemed like play.

The trainer clocked Black Lightning's time,
getting faster with ev'ry race.
It caught the eye of a Derby man
who said, "Come over to our place!"

Before the big Derby week,
   things started out in Keeneland—
Warm-up races to attract the racing fans
   and parades with a marching band.

The Derby town was one big party,
seven days of happy disorder—
With steamboat races and bright balloons,
celebrations on ev'ry corner.

The crowd gathered early at Churchill Downs
the first weekend in May.
The fillies race, then the main event
scheduled for Saturday.

The bugler from his lofty station
blew his long familiar call.
The racers in anticipation
prepared to give their all.

Gaston then joined the grand parade,
a strut from paddock to post—
The one last chance to show the the crowd
the team who had the most.

Then Black Lightning was away,
he left the post in a dash.
Only a blur to the eye
and he was gone in a flash.

The great steed ran like the wind—
he left the field behind,
Except for one approaching filly,
the fairest of her kind.

The gallant Cajun steed
had nothing if not class.
He politely stepped aside
and let the filly pass.

Gaston went back to the swamp
  and Black Lightning to his farm.
This strange pair in the future
  would cause racing no alarm.